This chilly quest
belongs to

Far away, in the cold north of the world . . .

SUPER FROZEN MAGIC FOREST

OXFORD

UNIVERSITY PRESS

The Super Happy Magic Forest had no defence
against the falling snow flakes.

The heroes were equipped and set off into the north.
Nothing would stand in their way.

Continuing north, they tried to blend in with the locals.

Before long, the game was up.
A chase was on.

But they couldn't run forever.

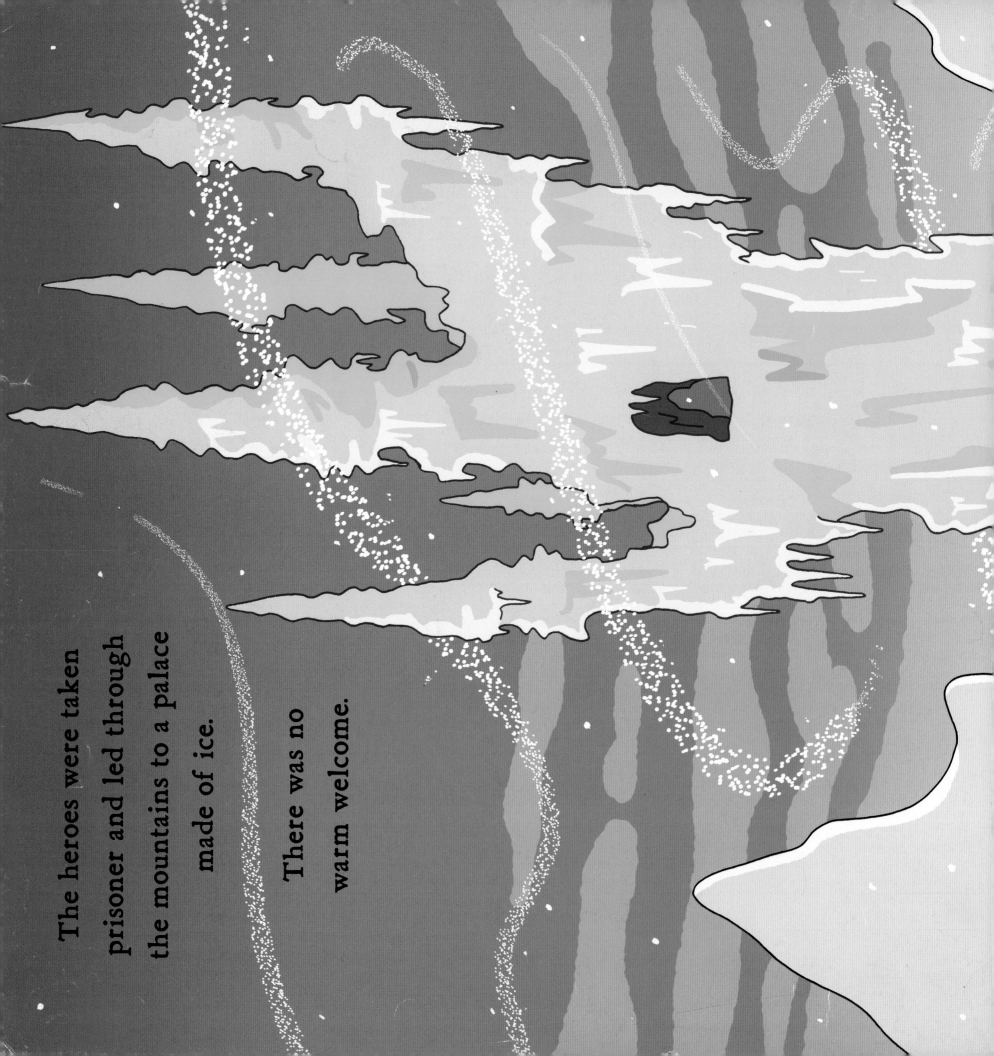

The heroes were taken prisoner and led through the mountains to a palace made of ice.

There was no warm welcome.

The Ice Queen's magic struck each of the heroes until only one remained.

Back in the Super Happy Magic Forest, the snow clouds began to clear and the sun shone brightly once more.

And once the rest of the heroes had thawed out,
they made their way home in double-quick time.

Where there was only one thing left to do . . .

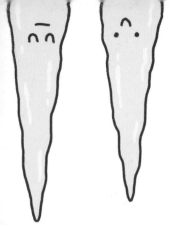

For Pete Marley, the quest giver.

And anyone who set sail with the Salty Dogs.

OXFORD
UNIVERSITY PRESS

Great Clarendon Street, Oxford OX2 6DP
Oxford University Press is a department of the University of Oxford.
It furthers the University's objective of excellence in research, scholarship,
and education by publishing worldwide. Oxford is a registered trade mark of
Oxford University Press in the UK and in certain other countries

Text and illustrations copyright © Matty Long 2018
The moral rights of the author and illustrator have been asserted
Database right Oxford University Press (maker)
First published 2018

British Library Cataloguing in Publication Data

Data available
ISBN: 978-0-19-274860-7 (paperback)

1 3 5 7 9 10 8 6 4 2

Printed in China

Paper used in the production of this book is a natural,
recyclable product made from wood grown in sustainable forests.
The manufacturing process conforms to the environmental
regulations of the country of origin.

With the snow long gone, tales of Herbert's
heroics spread through the Super Happy Magic Forest.
They were cherished for all time.